This book belongs to:

About this book:

When we are true to who we are, we shine.
This book was written to help children understand how
friendships can be complex and difficult, and how
sometimes, friends may not treat each other with the
kindness and respect we all deserve.

The goal of this book is to inspire, guide, and facilitate
change through discussion and inner reflection.

When we understand what real friendship entails and
what it should not be, then important discussions about
manipulation and controlling behaviours can happen.
Additional materials to extend the learning possibilities
through conversations about choices and responsibilities
are also available on our website.

Special thanks to Dr. Stephanie Margolese, who offered
valuable insight and suggestions based on her experience
as a clinical child psychologist.

www.plantlovegrow.com
©plantlovegrow 2018
©Elaheh Bos 2018

ISBN: 978-1985132405
ISBN: 1985132400

MILLIE, the Puppet

By Elaheh Bos

Millie liked to perform and be funny,
but only when no one was looking.

She was also quirky and witty.

She was oh so theatrical
and sometimes, a little magical...
But only for herself.

No one knew that Millie dreamed of being on stage,
because Millie was never on stage.
So when the spotlight was there,
Millie, too shy, never, ever was.

Katie, on the other hand, was not shy at all.

It was as if she was born on stage and always
seemed to know exactly what to do in the spotlight.

She loved the attention that came
with dazzling an audience.
She loved the applause as well, because it made her
feel special, as if she was the only star in the sky
and that everyone was admiring
how brightly she shone.

One day, while rehearsing a song,
Katie noticed Millie practicing
behind the curtains.

Katie had never
realized how funny Millie was.

Millie kept talking to herself behind the curtains
as if she was performing a show,
not aware that she was being watched.
After a few jokes, she sang a short song
before making her ukulele disappear in a puff
of magic. Millie was different and artistic
in a way Katie had never noticed.

Katie couldn't believe she had discovered Millie.

Katie moved closer to Millie.
"You should perform," she said.

"But I can't," Millie shrieked. "What if I freeze?"

Katie shook her head. "You won't."

"What if I faint?" Millie continued,
as she buried her face behind her paws.

"You won't," Katie replied.
"I'll help you be a star and then we can shine together."

Millie didn't need to be a star,
she just wanted to be herself.

But deep down inside the softness
of her belly and the fluffiness of her heart,
Millie had always dreamed of being on stage.
Just imagining herself making people smile
and laugh made her feel hopeful and happy.

She felt giddy and excited
at the idea that Katie would help her.
She knew that Katie was amazing on stage
and seemed so comfortable up there.

How could anything possibly go wrong
now that Katie was helping her?
Maybe she was finally ready to give the stage a try?

Katie picked her outfit.
Katie told her what song to sing.
Katie told her she shouldn't do her favourite
magic trick or tell her jokes.

Katie told her how to stand, and talk, and smile.
She told her what to say, how to nod,
and how to twist her tail into a heart.

Katie told her this... and that... and everything in between.

And when the night of Millie's performance arrived,
everything went according to Katie's plan.
Because of all her practice and hard work,
Millie did not freeze or stumble.
She was terrific on stage. She had done
everything Katie had asked because
she really wanted to learn from Katie.
The only problem was she didn't feel like Millie anymore.

And to Millie's surprise, Katie took all the credit,
as if she had been the one on stage that night.

And this was just the beginning of Katie's plans
for Millie...

"Maybe I can do my magic trick," Millie would suggest.
"And then I can sing one of my new songs?
It's really funny, just listen!"

"You have to do it my way," Katie answered instead,
dismissing this idea as she had rejected all of Millie's
other suggestions. "I discovered you," she added.

"But..." was all Millie managed.

"I know what's best," Katie continued, interrupting
and ignoring Millie's small protest.
"Just do what I tell you."

But...

"But..."
was all Millie
ever managed.

When Katie said jump, Millie jumped.
When Katie said smile, Millie smiled.
When Katie said be happy,
Millie pretended to be happy.

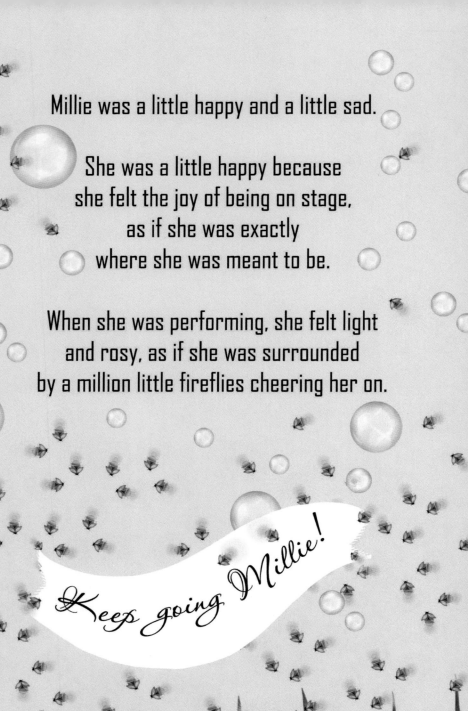

Millie was a little happy and a little sad.

She was a little happy because
she felt the joy of being on stage,
as if she was exactly
where she was meant to be.

When she was performing, she felt light
and rosy, as if she was surrounded
by a million little fireflies cheering her on.

Keep going Millie!

She was also sad
because she felt like a puppet
with Katie pulling the strings.

Millie wondered if maybe Katie was right.
Now that Katie had helped her,
would she always have to do what Katie wanted?

"I'm your friend," Katie often reminded her.
"I made you a star, so you have to do everyt[hing]
I say forever and ever."

That seemed like a very, very long time to M[illie.]

She was grateful that Katie had helped her b[ecause]
if it hadn't been for her she would still be hi[ding]
behind the stage. But the more Millie was on[stage]
the less she felt like herself.

This was a confusing and very sad way to be[cause]
Millie couldn't talk, give suggestions, make d[ecisions]
or even share how she felt anymore.

She had become Millie,
the puppet.

"This is what you should wear," Katie said
one morning as she handed Millie an outfit.

Millie couldn't believe her eyes.
It was a puppet costume.

Even when Millie told her she didn't want to wear it,
Katie didn't care and ignored her.

"You are lucky to have a friend like me.
I know what's best," was all Katie said to explain
why she got to make all the choices.

Millie started to wonder just how lucky she really was.

She looked at herself in the mirror.
She had become Katie's puppet
and that didn't make her feel special.

She didn't feel happy.

She didn't even feel excited to be part
of the biggest talent show at school.

"Friends help each other be themselves,"
Millie said quietly.

"I helped you be a star," Katie said as she frowned.
"I made you who you are."

"No," Millie said firmly as she handed the
puppet costume back to Katie. "I was always who I am.
You just wanted to pull my strings. I'm not your puppet
anymore."

Katie frowned in surprise. "But..."

Millie had been shaking inside as she said the words.
She had never stood up for herself before.
As good as it felt, it also felt scary and new.
It was like trying to walk in very big shoes and not
knowing whether each step she took would make
her fall. And yet, she felt brave and strong.
She was finally able to be herself again.

"Yes, you helped me," Millie said as calmly as she could.
"Thank you for that, but you are not a true friend.
Friends listen to and respect each other.
They don't get to make ALL the decisions."

"But..." was all Katie said as she watched Millie
walk away.

Even though Millie was still scared
of performing on stage,
she went on with the show.

She picked her own clothes,
sang her funny new song,
and even did a little magic trick.

Although she wished things
had worked out differently with Katie,
she knew that being alone
was better than being with someone
who only pretended to be her friend,
so she could pull her strings.

Keep going Millie!

ELODIE AND I
TRYING ON SOME WEIRD POSES...

**ADDING BUBBLES
TO MY MAGIC ACT**

By being true to herself,
Millie was a real star.

She attracted new friends
who liked her just the way she was.

WITH LEILA AFTER
THE MUSIC FESTIVAL

WITH KATIE, WE WON!
WE'RE NOT BESTIES, BUT WE RESPECT
EACH OTHER NOW AND THAT'S A START.
SECOND CHANCES AND ALL...

Discussion ideas:

MILLIE the Puppet

1. Why do you think the author used the example of the puppet in this book to talk about different friendship issues?

2. **Manipulation.**
Find the definition of the word and discuss whether it applies in this story. Share examples of other negative behaviors that can be found in unhealthy friendships.

3. Discuss whether you believe you have choices in the way you interact with friends.

4. Discuss what you can do if you see bullying, jealousy, or controlling behaviour between friends.

5. Discuss what you think about the message of this book and if you agree with it.

6. Discuss what "being a true friend" means to you.

Sometimes, we become targets for bullies and find ourselves in a difficult situation. Read the suggestions together of what you can do and discuss with your class or someone you trust what might be other options.

You may feel like you are a target and are being picked on because something is wrong with you. It is important to remember to be true to yourself and to try not to take the teasing personally or let the pain inside your heart.

Keep your head up high and be confident.
Don't let someone who is trying to intimidate you know that they are hurting you.
If they know that their words and actions are affecting you,
they will be more likely to continue.

Tell someone you trust. Start with your friends as you build up more courage to tell a teacher, parent, or another trusted adult.

Stand up to the bully if you can either on your own or with a friend or two. Tell them that you don't like it without using insults or making things worse. Remember that you are still responsible for your own actions and words.

Try to focus on the activities and people that bring you joy and what makes you unique and special.

Read the list of Cactus/Flower friends together.
Discuss if you feel you should change or add anything.
Add to the list of things that either a cactus or a flower might do.

Cactus friends
Get too close and you'll get hurt!

They may pretend to be your friend,
but they are not.
They make mistakes and may
pretend to apologize.
They pick on you or others.
They want to control you.
They ask you not to tell others
if they have hurt you.
They don't want you
to have other friends.
They don't let you have a say over things.
They say bad things about you
in front of you.
They say bad things about you
behind your back.
They hurt your feelings on purpose.
They make you feel bad
about the way you look.
They don't care about your opinion.
They like to get you in trouble.
They create stories
about you that are not true.
They make you feel miserable.
You don't feel safe
when they are around.

YOU are allergic
to cactus friends.

Flower friends
Everyone blooms together!

They genuinely care
about you as a friend.
They make mistakes
and apologize.
They are respectful of your feelings.
They like you as you are.
They make sure that you are safe.
They understand that sometimes
you want to play with other people.
You can work things out
when issues come up.
They will not tease you
if you tell them to stop.
They will talk to you directly
if there's a problem.
You can discuss together if you
have bruised each other's feelings.
They support you
and encourage you to be yourself.
They respect your opinion
even if it's different.
They like to play and have fun with you.
They tell the truth.
They make you feel good
about yourself.
They want to spend time with you.
You feel safe
with them around.

YOU want to bloom
with other flower friends.

We come in all shapes and sizes, with different abilities, talents, and challenges. Our experiences make us unique and allow us to share something different and special with each other.

When we can appreciate what we each have to offer and focus on helping each other out and learning from one another, we can start creating stronger friendships and making better choices.

Write down some of your qualities and what makes you unique.

Do the same for some of your friends and try to appreciate what makes each of you unique.

Books, journals, activity sheets, encouragement tools, support material and more...

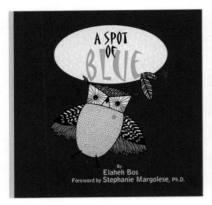

plant
love
gr❂w

www.plantlovegrow.com